World of Reading

LEVEL

RESCUE FROM JABBA'S PALACE

WRITTEN BY MICHAEL SIGLAIN

ART BY PILOT STUDIO

DISNEP

LUCASFILM
PRESS

Los Angeles • New York

All rights reserved. Published by Disney • Lucasfilm Press, an imprint of Disney
Book Group. No part of this book may be reproduced or transmitted in any form or
by any means, electronic or mechanical, including photocopying, recording, or by
any information storage and retrieval system, without written permission from the
publisher. For information address Disney • Lucasfilm Press, 1101 Flower Street,
Glendale, California 91201.

Printed in the United States of America

First Edition, April 2015

3 5 7 9 10 8 6 4 2

Library of Congress Control Number: 2014937082

FAC-029261-15072

ISBN 978-1-4847-0501-8

SUSTAINABLE
FORESTRY
INITIATIVE

Certified Sourcing

www.sfiprogram.org
SFI-01415

Han Solo was in trouble.

He had been captured by
Darth Vader and frozen.

Then he was given to a
bounty hunter named
Boba Fett.

Boba Fett worked for the
vile gangster Jabba the Hutt.
Han owed Jabba money but
did not pay him back.

Boba Fett's job was to
bring Han to Jabba.
If Jabba could not get
Han's money, he would get Han!

But Han's friends had a plan
to rescue him.
C-3PO and R2-D2
went to Jabba's palace.
They brought Jabba a
message from Luke.

Luke wanted to bargain
with Jabba to free Han Solo.
But Jabba refused.
He liked Han hanging on his wall
for all to see.

Jabba kept C-3PO in his court
and put R2-D2 on his sail barge.
Then another bounty hunter arrived.

This bounty hunter brought
Chewie to Jabba.
But this bounty hunter wasn't
really a bounty hunter at all.

The bounty hunter was
Princess Leia in disguise!
She had come to unfreeze Han!

Princess Leia freed Han,
but they could not escape
from Jabba the Hutt!

Jabba made Princess Leia
his slave and put Han
in the dungeon with Chewie.

Next Luke came to help.
He tried to talk to Jabba,
but Jabba wouldn't listen.

Jabba dropped Luke
into the rancor pit.

The rancor was a big monster.
Luke fought the rancor
and won!

This made Jabba very angry.
He told the heroes that
they would be dropped into
the Sarlacc pit and never escape.
Now Han and his friends were
really in trouble!

Everyone boarded Jabba's
sail barge for the trip
through the desert.

Jabba was going to make the heroes
walk the plank and fall
into the mouth of the Sarlacc.

Jabba's men moved Luke into place.
Luke stood at the edge of the plank.
He signaled to R2-D2, and then . . .

Luke jumped off the plank!
But he didn't fall into the pit.
Luke flipped through the air
just as R2-D2 shot an object
into the sky!

Luke landed back on the skiff
and caught the object.
It was his new lightsaber!

And it was green!

Luke battled Jabba's men
and freed Han and Chewie.
That was when Boba Fett
landed on the scene.

Luke fought Boba Fett.
Then Han hit Boba Fett's
jet pack, causing him to fly away.

Boba Fett crashed into the sail barge and fell into the Sarlacc pit.

Inside the sail barge,
Jabba was very, very mad.
He didn't notice Princess Leia
standing behind him.

Princess Leia used a big chain to
defeat the vile gangster.
And thanks to R2-D2, they escaped.

On the top deck of the sail barge,
Luke fought the rest of Jabba's men.
Princess Leia joined him, and they
fired the cannon at the deck.

They swung to safety and
joined their friends on the skiff.
Jabba's sail barge exploded!

Thanks to Han Solo's friends,
he had been rescued,
and Jabba the Hutt
had been defeated.